TAP TO PLAY!

Salina Yoon

BALZER + BRAY

An Imprint of HarperCollinsPublishers

Hi!
I'm BLIP.

I need to reach that
bar to win the game.
Can you help me?

How do I get from HERE

to THERE?

5 4 3 2 1

If I win, I get a
SURPRISE!

I've got it.
I'll BOUNCE up!
Could you shake the book
so I can bounce?
Go ahead. Shake!

WARNING: I bleep under stress.

NOT SO
FAST!

5 4 3 2 1

BLEEP!

Bounce it slower, please!

That's better.
But now I feel dizzy.

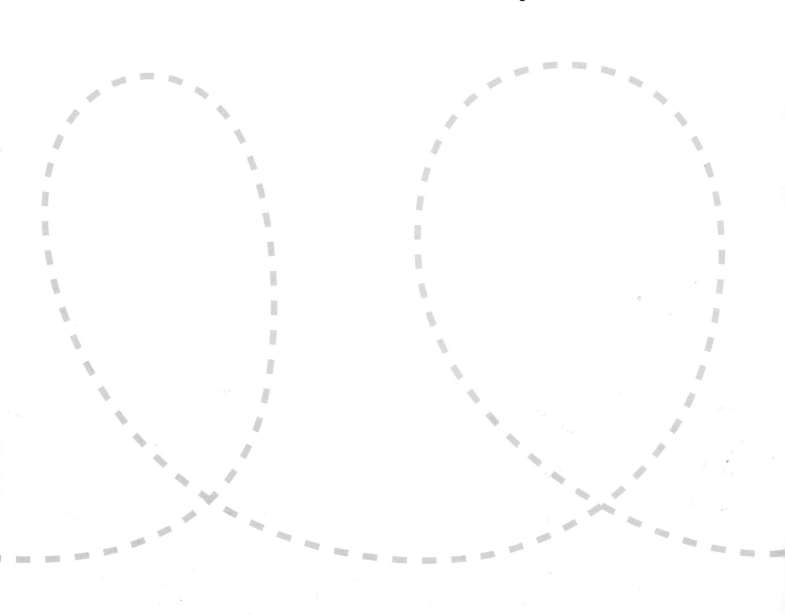

5 4 3 2 1

**How about turning
me over and I'll
aim for the bar?**

Hm. That didn't work.

BLEEP!

Could you stand the
book up straight?
I need to get down.

Maybe you can tilt
me to the right.

WHOA!

BLEEP!

4 3 2 1

TOO FAR!

Tilt me to the left!

AHHH!

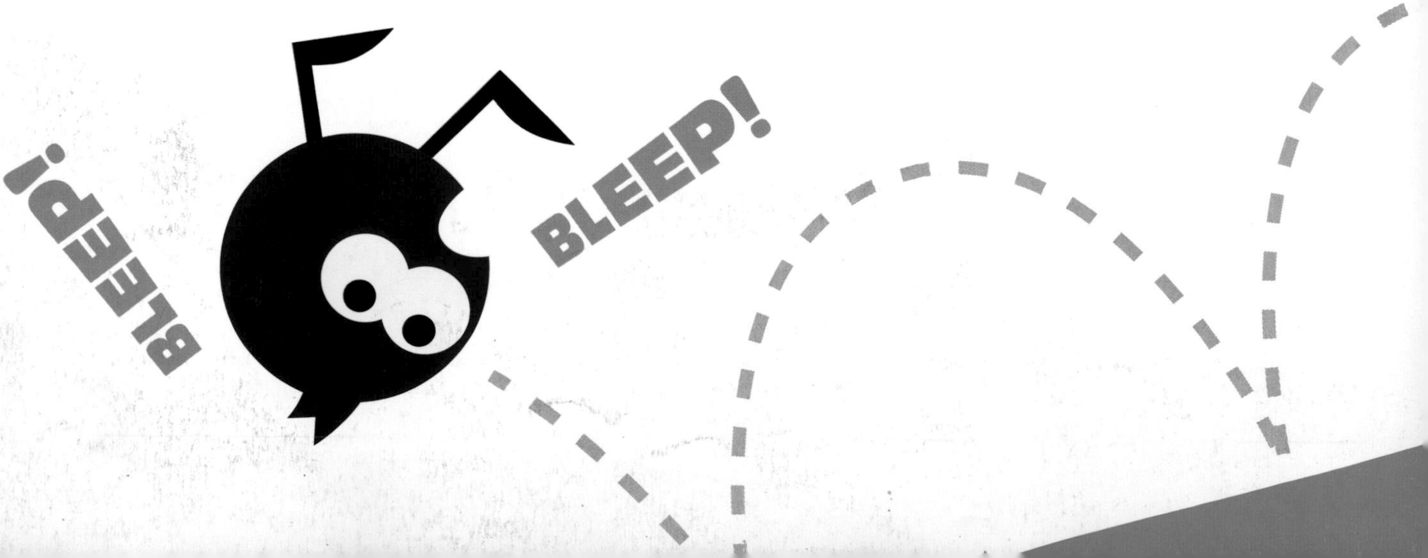

NO MORE TILTING!

I need a fresh start.
Tap me twice
and shout,

"BLIP!"

OUCH! Not that hard!

Tap me twice again—
gently this time!—
and whisper,

"BLIP!"

There! That did the trick!
What? Why are you laughing at me?

Ha-ha, very funny. If you tickle my foot, my head will grow back.

Ha!

Ha!

Ha!

Ha!

It worked!

**But I still need
to win the game
before time's up.**

Hm. If I could grow bigger,
I might be able to reach the bar.

Will you help me grow?

Just fill up your mouth with air
and HOLD IT!

BLEEP!

2 1

Now I'm TOO big!
BLOW OUT!

WHEW!

Now tap on my shadow
to get me back in position.

I KNOW!

I have the perfect idea!

1

Could you flap the book open and closed as fast as you can? **HURRY!**

Hey, it's

working!

KEEP FLAPPING!

GOOD JOB!

We won the game!

But what's that?

It's my surprise!

Can you knock on
the door and open it
S - L - O - W - L - Y?

GULP.

KNOCK TO PLAY

A NEW FRIEND!

Do you want
to play?

YES!

For Cyndi and Robin, my best players
—Blip

Balzer + Bray is an imprint of HarperCollins Publishers.

Tap to Play!
Copyright © 2014 by Salina Yoon
All rights reserved. Manufactured in China.

ISBN 978-0-06-228684-0

The artist used Adobe Illustrator to create the digital illustrations for this book.
Typography by Rachel Zegar
14 15 16 17 18 SCP 10 9 8 7 6 5 4 3 2 1

First Edition